For L and P, two big J's and little n and I
— Steve Roslonek and Anand Nayak

For Susie
— David Sim

The
SHAPE
SONG
swingalong

Written and sung by
STEVESONGS

Illustrated by
DAVID SIM

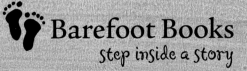

Barefoot Books
Step inside a story

I have a shape collection and I use it to create
Anything I want to see or be or do or make.
Is it work? Is it play? Is it music? Is it art?

With my shape collection all I need to do is start

square,
square,
square,
square,

triangle,
triangle ...

I drew a city with
big skyscrapers,

I drew people in the streets,

It started on the paper with a line, line, circle, circle, circle,

square, square, square, square, triangle, triangle...

I drew boats out on the water,

I drew a castle on the sand,
I drew a beachside waterslide,
Oh, what a ride!

And I never even had to stand in line, line, circle, circle, circle, square, square, square, square, triangle, triangle, triangle . . .

I drew a party in the park,
The DJ was a monkey,

Everybody there was dancing,
But no one was as funky ...

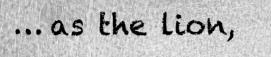

...as the lion,

line, circle, circle, square, square, square, square, triangle, triangle ...

ROAR!

Can you dance like a shape,
Then change into another?
That's a funny move to make!
Show your sister or your brother.

Here at the Shape Song Swingalong show
Come on everybody, let's sing it together!

We can do the line, line, circle, circle,

We make shapes in the day

And when the lights go out

We make shapes while we sleep
Because we're always dreaming about

...lines, lines, circles, circles, squares, squares, squares, squares, triangles, triangles, line, line, circle, circle, square, square, square, triangle, triangle, line, Line...

Barefoot Books
2067 Massachusetts Ave
Cambridge, MA 02140

Barefoot Books
294 Banbury Road
Oxford, OX2 7ED

First published in Great Britain by Barefoot Books, Ltd
and in the United States by Barefoot Books, Inc in 2011
All rights reserved

Graphic design by Penny Lamprell, Lymington, UK
Reproduction by B & P International, Hong Kong
Printed in China on 100% acid-free paper by Printplus, Ltd
This book was typeset in Soupbone, Circus Mouse, Roger and Chalkduster
The illustrations were prepared in gouache, acrylics and pastels

ISBN 978-1-84686-671-5

British Cataloguing-in-Publication Data:
a catalogue record for this book is available from the British Library

Library of Congress Cataloging-in-Publication Data
is available under LCCN 2011015461

3 5 7 9 8 6 4 2

Text copyright
© 2011 by SteveSongs
Illustrations copyright
© 2011 by David Sim
The moral rights of SteveSongs
and David Sim have been asserted
The song and lyrics were written by
Steve Roslonek and Anand Nayak

Recorded and mixed at Moo Moo House,
Easthampton, MA
SteveSongs appears courtesy of PBSKids
Animation by Karrot Animation, London, UK

Barefoot Books
step inside a story